THE
FAERIE
DEVOURING

THE
FAERIE
DEVOURING

CATHERINE
LALONDE

Translated by Oana Avasilichioaei

Book*hug
Toronto, 2018
Literature in Translation Series

FIRST ENGLISH EDITION

Published originally under the title: *La dévoration des fées* © Catherine Lalonde & Le Quartanier, Montreal, 2017

English translation copyright © 2018 Oana Avasilichioaei

The production of this book was made possible through the generous assistance of the Canada Council for the Arts and the Ontario Arts Council. Book*hug also acknowledges the support of the Government of Canada through the Canada Book Fund and the Government of Ontario through the Ontario Book Publishing Tax Credit and the Ontario Book Fund.

Canada Council   Conseil des Arts   Funded by the   Financé par le
for the Arts   du Canada   Government   gouvernement
                                      of Canada   du Canada

ONTARIO ARTS COUNCIL
CONSEIL DES ARTS DE L'ONTARIO
an Ontario government agency
un organisme du gouvernement de l'Ontario

We acknowledge the financial support of the Government of Canada through the National Translation Program for Book Publishing, an initiative of the *Roadmap for Canada's Official Languages 2013-2018: Education, Immigration, Communities*, for our translation activities.

Book*hug acknowledges the land on which it operates. For thousands of years it has been the traditional land of the Huron-Wendat, the Seneca, and most recently, the Mississaugas of the Credit River. Today, this meeting place is still home to many Indigenous people from across Turtle Island, and we are grateful to have the opportunity to work on this land.

Library and Archives Canada Cataloguing in Publication

Lalonde, Catherine, 1974–
[Dévoration des fées. English]
The faerie devouring / Catherine Lalonde ; Oana Avasilichioaei, translator.
— First English edition.

(Literature in translation series)
Translation of: La dévoration des fées.
Issued in print and electronic formats.

ISBN 978-1-77166-427-1 (softcover)
ISBN 978-1-77166-428-8 (HTML)
ISBN 978-1-77166-429-5 (PDF)
ISBN 978-1-77166-430-1 (Kindle)

I. Avasilichioaei, Oana, translator II. Title. III. Title: Dévoration des fées.
English. IV. Series: Literature in translation series
PS8573.A38345D4813 2018   C843'.54   C2018-904274-5
                                               C2018-904275-3

Printed in Canada

I

"(I speak like a grandmother)"

She said it from the get-go, when in the beginning was the word, when the very first words existed, the first she hearkened to in her life. Cruel precious revelations, gospel truths, migraine inducing, inaugural gift of the wicked faerie godmother magically brewed by faerie fingers ladyfingers: five words, five, like poison in the ear, like fledglings of misfortune, ponderous, prophetic, oracular; snake oil liniment and the whole kit and caboodle, and in her black heart a future spindle sharpened.

She said it. The grandmother said it. After the clamour of flesh, after the bloody harvest of the mound—liver, spleen, entrails, adorable arteries—the little mound more torn out than pushed, uprooted by the neighbour's skilled hands, Wilfred Thomassin the daughter, human forceps and sweaty expertise in the clammy chamber. She said it while the mother lay dying of too much blood and loss; and of spilling, becoming liquid agony. The grandmother said it so that they knew it in advance, before the morbid bloodless face, before the melting morphology that rock-a-bye baby, only the first will hear this common tune, for when mama breaks, the cradle will fall, and down will come baby, first and last, cradle and all.

There came silence. When the spent mother's face turned inside out like a glove, her human countenance howled outside herself, reduced for a split second to strident screams and lips, acrobatic decibels, then lips and silence silence silence; hair eyes nose teeth mouth fallen to the wayside, charms of a bracelet useless in this carnage, the string of the face broken right off and its pearls swallowed in silence. The spent mother's face, ravished, reduced to living tissue; visage become vagina; while from below the fresh face emerged in sublime agony, shat out, brand new. A fresh branchiole in the infinite genealogy of matryoshka dolls that suck their faces, like serpents, by eating their own tails.

She said it. After the scream that sounded the passage to being, as the death knell tolled, as the ridiculous squealing heralded life beginning, she said it; just after the air dance, in the chill of boiling oil that makes howling flesh actually alive, struck down by the horrible harshness of light—terrible winds, sounds, uncocooned sensations—once the thing and sublime agony expired, when the wailing fell silent, she said it.

The words came in response to the soothed screams when in the water gently warmed on the back burner they placed the refuse—the born thing uprooted rather than delivered, this rump not yet slapped and hatched too soon, this forced living thing, dragged outside the fresh-water cage, with unlimited lungs (air going in, from outside inside, a sensation of rusted revolving doors and crushed glass), eyes full of pus, all vernix, precerebral palmate paws, prehuman earthworm—she said it while outside the breaths, races, forced and anxious foolish laughs of the four others plus one (who only half counted) pierced the walls for an instant, while they began hearing beyond the cedar panelling, beyond the casket of the dying mother, a syncopated life resounding, beating, beating, beating wholeheartedly, continually, as it gets used so used to being.

She said it surrounded by the circle of women. Five words, five, as though under the influence of laurel poked and torched, she said it knowing in advance, while Luciana Matriciana drew the sheet to erase white with white the flour face music and milk of the mother dead forevermore. She said it amid the smoke and crackling wood, in the first moment warmth pleasure when the small fry was plunged in water—water, amazing discovery!—at the exact temperature at which it would then remain, this flesh come too soon, in the second drawer of the wood stove, under constant surveillance and quicksilver eye, for some two or three weeks depending on weight.

Weeping for her daughter, her only one, her Snow bled white she said it, and the crown of thorns banded her lips from then on always plainly Gramma. From then on always, a grandmother old forevermore, old of mouth and all around. From this source, five words fell out, branded in lead, five that slipped out, lost; as though wept, pearled, one by one, as drops of blood—or tears—would have done if she still could.

She said it, Gramma said it:

Fuck.

It's a girl.

"Tell your daughters not to follow my example."

Wilfred Thomassin the daughter is there. She costs a pretty penny, Gramma says. She's worth her weight in gold, instinctively opens the wood stove drawer, anticipating the cries. Keeps an eye on the thermometer, throws on another log or stokes the embers, even lets her suck cow milk off her callused fingers. Nipples are for the rich. Rock-a-bye baby slurps the taste of hair leather dung soil, then gets the runs of jaundice. Three times she gets it, and the sprite toughs it out. The sprite—the name sticks. She fattens up. She's hard-headed.

In her cast-iron and echo chamber, the third drawer of the wood stove, the sprite contents herself with her thumb, the taste of milk and the nearby fire, as though fastened to her mother's fire, as though still inside. A house full of squeals, four cowboys and one who loafs around—the one who only half counts. Sounds reach her from afar: life hushed by metal and isolation. Life runs parallel, arrives in bits and pieces, drop by drop, so already memory, already lagging behind; muffled sonar, pulsar from limbs to limbic system. The dough goes in and comes out of the right-side drawer, next-door neighbour, rises in the ideal warmth, doubles in size, slowly swelling up just like the sprite sucking on leather and lard. It smells of wheat and burnt birch. She gets attached to the warmth, the sleet of embers, the scree of cinders resonating in the wood bunker. The explosions of branches that fart as they burn are her lullabies, songs saying love, my pretty baby, my sweet li'l baby, my sweet sweet girl.

They take her out twenty-one days later. Swaddled in coarse woollen blankets, she is warmed up by the handwoven cloth. If she toughs it out, she'll join the ranks. The grandmother puts her to bed in the commode, bottom drawer—from drawer to drawer, she adjusts, it's her cradle—among the hooked rugs moth-eaten for the visitation. The brat hangs on to the front of the drawer, gives her his molar slobber and first words. The mongoloid sleeps on the floor, on duty like a good watchdog, sings if necessary, howls at the moon when she cries. As if I needed this, Gramma says.

She joins the ranks, extends the line of genealogy and among the urchins penned up on the floor for the washing-up she is flesh among flesh. A rump no more, nor gristle, just more of same. Same as the brood of mouths to feed: JJ—John-Jude—and Luke in full growth spurt, two. Matthew the redhead, three; then the brat who still eats like a bird thank God, four; and the mongoloid, who counts for nothing but eats for two. And the sprite. The sprite who will soon shift to solids, solid food's pricey, that makes six. Six, naked after the washing-up, swarming like white grubs surprised under the turnip crate. And her? The same. Shits the same. Sucks the same, pisses the same, bleeds the same. The diaper on her ass tells you nothing. But you know it, Gramma says, you know it.

The door creaks upon winter, and the dry nor'easter scrapes the sprite's cheekbones, rides bareback on her zygomatic arches. Oh. She squints her eyes and the rolls of her face, white spots and lights linger beneath her eyelids, my God, it's full of stars! The Wilfred Thomassins mother and daughter take her out for the first time. The world. Outside. The sprite is bundled into an onion, like some fragile porcelain: eight layers, cotton raw wool fur, they wonder as they step through the door if it wouldn't be best to add two or three more, but hop! it'll do, the sprite's tough. The Wilfred Thomassins pass her between them like a hot potato and laugh at her face shrivelled like a glistening grub. The sprite's as light as a feather, but the storm has left its mark. Legs lifted high and exhausted after ten steps. Almost an hour to reach the Old Crone's house, face the mother of serpents, the one who's been spinning her wheel for many moons.

The Old Crone says it, among the chastity stones and black veils, the nooks and crannies of the recluse she says it, with her used mouth, five words let loose, light as ether, five that fly off one by one, like blown kisses would. She says it, five words: Oh, the lovely li'l queen!, with her toothless mouth and it doesn't fall on deaf ears.

The Old Crone licks the ball of her thumb with her tongue, draws a sign of the cross on the sprite's brow, takes her in her arms and raptures her out of the rest of the world, time in her rocking chair to hand down her godmother gifts. The Old Crone sings them, sings lullabies, songs in 6/8 saying love, my pretty baby, my li'l queen, my sweet li'l baby, my sweet sweet girl, and verses of the six unnamed male stillborns, of the two late-born maids maidens. The Wilfred Thomassins take up the little bundle and bring her back to the fold, puffing and huffing and laughing like mules under the weight of the snow.

A return to the warmth, the blur. It's the sprite's life, who toughs it out without knowing she toughs it. Hot-cold, full-empty, wet-dry, raw-tender. When the emptiness engulfs her, she sucks on a corner of the hooked rug, swallows a moth, devours with her naked gums, constantly famished. It's simple, the dream of the childheart: baba mama baba Snow though limp though lifeless, eat Wilfred Thomassin the daughter's cow fingers, eat your hand tra-la-la-la. In this baby ogre devouring, she eats her echo, and the fire and spark, and keeps the other for tomorrow.

What does a baby dream if not something better than us? Still engulfed in images, in the tidal wave of the original encephalon, with no barrage or capacity, still not far from emptiness and nonbeing, the sprite is buoyant, suspended as though in her mother's ghostly limbs, levitating from one place to another, from one world to the other by the grown-ups' enchanted grasp. Modelling is underway: suck well, little baby, suck fingers of milk, suck directly to the brain. The virgin heart beats in her big soft head. The fontanelle pumps, absorbs hair and worse, to the rhythm of the suction, and the sprite closes her eyes, hears the splendour music from the mouth of her dead mother, dead for a long time now, a long time in terms of milk, a long time in terms of hunger.

A miniature. An excerpt, a reduction. The sprite is a wee thing, more a woman's spit than minifaerie, plagued by infinite electric spasms. Her movements are epileptic wigglywags, but no one's there to aaaaaahooooooooh! her inductions. Like an empress, she's carried about on the palanquin of crossed hands and arms—watch the head! watch the slack, the soul's marrow!—those of Thomassin the daughter, Luciana Matriciana and JJ, the eldest, those of the mongoloid. But never in Gramma's arms. Gramma, hands on hips, watches her from afar, doesn't touch her except when forced to. The sprite, sausaged up in ripped raw cotton, nods off, neck like a broken heron's, sleeps like a log anywhere with no night night sleep tight don't let the bedbugs bite. She wakes slowly, very slowly, teleported: I flew! she will say later, waking up somewhere else from where she fell asleep.

The sprite starts crawling more and more, faster and faster. She grows stronger, her hands thrust and push the floor, and her head lifts up—less and less wormlike, more and more snakelike. Change in level, perspective: she moves from ground to horizon, and her heart heaves, led by the desire to look them in the eyes, JJ watching her, the mongoloid laughing, Gramma grumbling. The sprite builds muscles from the attempts and tumbles. Pushing = seeing, and possible footholds and grips. Falling = being with oneself, in the rumbling bowels of anti-social digestion. She explores, St. Vitus's dancer, she crawls about, and increasingly vertebrate, she slips her twig-fingers between the pine floorboards, scrapes soot, frass, broken rosary beads, a thousand wonders and dust mites, brings them, pure reflex, to her mouth, baba dead mama dust baba

eat the snow-white absence, eat, three times her hand will grow back, and keep the other you never know for tomorrow.

Gramma says it, when she thinks the brood's sleeping, when she's hatching them: John-Jude the adopted eldest, JJ her pride and joy; the brat Peter-Joseph, JJ's son, JJ, the precocious papa; James the mongoloid, adopted with; her own Luke; and the late-born Matthew— and Snow the fiery floating phantom, once long-awaited and now so

absent,

Gramma says it, and it doesn't fall on deaf ears.

"ugliness brings forth beauty"

The sprite barely stands on two legs. She spends her days clutching JJ's ankles when he's not on horseback, nose smack dab in the stench of dung, and the rest of the time hooked on the mongoloid's smiles. She falls plumb down, her buttocks hitting the wood floor with a hard thud. The fingernail faerie never drops by to file her grime. Spends hours with her mouth open to the four winds, corners split south-north-east from happiness, dying of laughter, jaws joyous from being open to all: wind, warbles, mosquitoes and the mongoloid's tickles. She scampers in a precarious balance, falls like an acrobat, rolling ass over head. She'd take pride in it if she knew what she was doing. That time will come, and come quick, since time like Snow sparkles effervescent with absence.

Washing day. The last li'l ones are lined up for the sponge-down. Far from the wood stove, the sprite squirms like a worm, tickled by chills. The washtub is on the burner, the washrag, rough, it's to toughen you up, child, I won't have any wimps in this family. The redhead is old enough to wipe his own ass: Gramma gives him his washrag. Then she goes down the military ranks of fresh fannies. In the middle, the brat is rubbed raw and swallowed in smooches, now lapped by the rag, now by the tongue; so plump, so pudgy with cellulite you could eat him up. Yum-yum and snuggly-cuddly; a lick of the rag, a smear of drool, and laughter, this cascade of two and three quarters years is contagious. Gramma would smile if she still could. The sprite babbles, also ready, always ready, flesh willingly chilled, my what biiiiiiiiig teeth you have, and her turn comes only with cold water splashed on the face from afar. Which doesn't keep her from babbling or laughing.

The sprite sleeps with her eyes open, her arms and long legs dangling outside the drawer. Gramma pesters: close your eyes or the bogeyman will get you. Wicked child, bad omen. Treats her. Lambert Syrup. Leeches, crucifixes, poultices. Sweating. Cod liver oil. Bloodletting. The sprite giggles, tickled. Beef marrow ointment, fresh egg yolks, purging screams—in the cedar casing, all is absorbed. Nothing helps, except the sprite triples in size like bread dough, like a mushroom: and the dream always escapes her pupils and falls bruised on the floor, in puddles, cascades, soaks the hooked rug, the wood floor, trickles between the boards, rejoins the soil, humus, mycelium. Gramma sticks her foot in it at the crack of dawn, the time for kneading dough. She rages, swears, kneels down on all fours, sponges it dry. Gotta find some wood to make her a bed, she grumbles, beaver budgeting in her mind, trying to figure out how to save on hinges and nails.

Snow sparkles with absence. The pain gnaws at the tough sprite and Gramma, the erasure of this mother barely maid, maiden so soon erased, her dissolution flour milk sweet clover; the scorching volatility in everything that is snow-white, even here, an

absence.

So then, the rot starts in the mouth, Gramma will say. Spoiling for the first word, when in the beginning was the word, the others' gift of hearkening, after the drooling gums and the vocalizations of a skinned cat. When she says them, the first, the very first words of her life.

The sprite hears. The cracked bowl of her head is a new echo chamber. The sounds, born inside or out, bounce off the sutured ivory, transform from songs and savage gibberish into sense and significance; and one suddenly flares, like a firefly in the milky zenith—a flame, a flash of lightning, and understanding is a wonder. In her skull the very first word emerges from this glimmering glow, the first hearsay of her life, etched by the wicked faerie godmother in the intimate ripples of bone, a note, one syllable that grows from the occiput to her lips, this primal F of branches burgeoned from mother to daughter, a muffled and genetic fricative—first and last, cradle and all—from the depth to the surface and the sudden F shoots out, shaping a rolling tunnel of the lower lip, tracing for a split second a primal strident F U.

No, the sprite says instead, cheating fate. Right off, it's said done written, in the mother alphabet, in invisible ink in the spirals of sweet clover. Right off, written in cranial whiteness and velum, prophetic croaking of the fledgling before her time. First word, rootword. No.

That's where she lives, Gramma will say, in this small slit thing, toughly on two legs, the glowing ill crux of the balphabet path. The oracle, deafening, more flawed than foretold. That's where she lives the absence: even stones have mothers, and dead mothers their memories. A little tart, definite vagina cocked at the end of a line, genealogical brood of grandmothers mothers daughters martyrs, women to sweat out the race, like her, with three adopted children—JJ the precocious papa and his adored brat, and the mongoloid who only half counts— and her own fatherless two, with the sprite, fuck that makes six, would've been seven with the absent Snow, and her hands would've been useful and needed and loved. Like Violet's, Violet the almost twin sister, now so dead, so far, died birthing half a man. Gramma sees it. She too will fall.

Her own big little bed, the sprite's. Hers, hers alone. Long enough that she can grow into it. The sprite keeps her stinky doll, the one with the iron eyes and a mane of horsehair, secreted under the mattress far away from the rest of the stuff. Painted grains of rice, marbles of dry peas, spears of blue jay feathers, branches, nests and leaves waters and worlds spit up by the forest and pirated for toys can very well fly up into a tarantella and disappear, Close sesame, you just need to reinvent them. But the doll. The doll. Ever since the sprite kidnapped her from the stand where she used to sit smartly, ornamental, she must protect her from ogres, dark shadows and embers; embers, even

absent ones.

The sprite whispers to her at midnight to soothe her with lullabies of filched dolls flying dolls, songs saying love, my li'l queen, my sweet li'l baby, my sweet sweet girl.

John-Jude Luke James Matthew Peter-Joseph the sprite. All the progeny in one breath, in order of appearance in Gramma's eyes. A playful
six-headed six-tailed monster. Six fledglings, their skin rough from
rolling in the grass, six nestlings nestled on her tongue, hindering
her from biting speaking eating. All with their beaks open, one and
all, but the grandmother is alone in her pangs of yearning breathing.

The six-headed monster scampers around, turns into a tornado, a wild herd, a caterpillar of linked legs: the spritely papoose bareback on the mongoloid, the brat behind putting on airs, the older ones jumping over the hurdle, turning a sharp corner. Hay in their hair, burrs on their calves, scratches and roses on their cheeks, barely muddy, they sow seeds, pine cones, slugs and disorder in their wake. End up having to race, otherwise they'll eat their black oats and summer dog stew cold. Or they'll slip under the table, and that's that hereabouts. Gramma looks at the drooling gathering, contemplates the Little Chinese Girls River, kittens in burlap sacks, mountain landslides, pine forest fires. She daydreams of the fountain of torments, water of little terrors—child's water of eternal dodos—reflects at herself in her old head, sees herself there; she, a big dying princess, infanta drowned in the dishwater, one plate at a time. She feeds nightmares with Hail Marys and faeries to keep scraping by, scraping by, surviving, first and last, cradle and all, surviving.

The dirty crockery on the long, long table, hewn along with its benches out of hard beams by a man's hands. The bowls piled in rickety towers of grime. The forks stuck defiantly in the wood's fibre, boys playing games like dogs. Gramma's on the scent, all around, underneath, on the walls, to wipe the stains, blastings, the splattered mess of fertilizer the cerberus of John-Jude Luke James Matthew Peter-Joseph the sprite wolfs down, this bone flour that makes them grow like quackgrass. Goddamn daily cavalcade, goddamn stampede. Gramma fantasizes about witches' brooms, would damn her soul for a magical tool, a flying dishcloth, soap. For any power against the pulsing and obstinate backwash of the chaos, be it on the rag loony. A girl's job, she tells herself, a goddamn girl's job, once more muzzling the urge to chuck the plates, imagining the cow-children at the trough, the water, the honey, even the Honeycomb box, the penniless pigstyless piglets feeding on stone soup and mud roast. She's eager for the sprite to put on some weight, leaven her breasts, put yeast on her hips, for the monthlies to anchor her, cotton on her ass barefoot in the kitchen, hands in the dough halter around her neck; she's eager for the sprite to reach, at last, her made woman's life; her woman's life made of blood and dishwater.

Gramma loses her footing in the eternal macabre dance of the vanished Snow, the urchins and objects. Blasted things, always in everything; and the two adopted sons, the mongoloid, her own fatherless two, and the sprite. A single shoe, cups, nails, hellish wooden swords, sock monkeys and mismatched stockings, lumps of homemade soap, forks, crumbs sand magical stones and scarabs, moved by six puppeteers beset by the impulse to cause maximum disorder. Even the doll has disappeared, Snow's doll when she was little before she was a mother before she was dead. Gramma's heart clamps up, hollers Close the door, the flies! Pick up your stuff, I'm not gonna tell you thrice! Worse than a pack of hyenas, who'd've thought! She steps on a rosary bead, swears, opens the door to holler John-Jude Luke James Matthew Peter-Joseph the sprite! Come eat, I'm not gonna tell you twice!

What about the men? Male hands? Her husband? Breeches, penknife and deadwood. All dead. All died too soon. Her father died on the log drive. The six brothers before her, stillborn one after another in the Old Crone's belly. The brother-in-law died of TB. The husband died like all men not fully come back from the war. The cousins of smallpox, the grocer of shame at the stake, the pastor of verseworms, the others of famine, in the Little Chinese Girls River, of consumption injections warm piss and pity; the neighbour of Irish whisky, the one to the west of adulterated drink and revelry. Died of dying, like all men. Like flies, like cowards, like all men all the others.

She sees her, Gramma sees her. While she pursues her infinitesimal suicide, Palmolive bubbles in the veins, getting chapped hands in the dishwater—the cuticles and tips of the nails flaking off first—she sees through the window above the sink the sprite walking through the frame mountains chasms cows pigs progeny, running in the brood, her mane almost horizontal, running and running as though yesterday already came and went, breathless. There she goes gallopin' 'tween the bowls and lumps of grits; there she is spritely 'tween the pissing spout and the spoons clanging metal against metal in tune with her stampede; and again, a pantomime imitating you'd die of laughter the crown of thorns of Gramma's lips. The sprite, who thinks herself so tough with her dragon collection and secreted stinky doll, when she's only yay high. A babbler with knock knees and words constantly slippin' and slidin', and that you'd expect to trip up here.

Only two are left naked and standing in the washtub of tepid water. The redhead can already wash himself in the Little Chinese Girls River, and that's a big help, Gramma says. The brat goes through the twister of washrag and smooches; the sprite soaked on her feet, chilled to the bone in the biting dusk, is unwilling to rub the goosebumps on her skin. No fire before September, Gramma says, instructing, scrubbing, overseeing, and rub with more force, otherwise you'll turn to bait. The sprite wriggles like the fleas the rough washrag expels from her skin. A circus frolics on her stomach, in her armpits that shadow some fresh fuzz, only a month old. She shivers in the tingling breeze, giggles, and her staccato laughter is contagious. The brat catches on, adds his own hysterical hiccups, kicks up his heels; falls dramatically ass in the plate feet in the air; his washtub tips over, and the grimy water spills, spreads slowly on the floor. Gramma tightens her lips: run for your life, it's her witchy mouth. She snatches the brat with one claw, drags him, grabbing a wooden spoon on the way, throws him face down on the table. Spanks him. The sprite squirms under the brat's cries, her long white legs stiffen. And she sees. The sprite sees. Gramma'd crack a smile if she still could.

The sprite's more handy with her slingshot and penknife than the knitting needles. She bombards the noggins of fledglings with stones; with a bit of luck, a red star bursts inside, expansion of a parallel universe, a small school of death: crow drops dead, neck broken, a narrow trickle of red liquid draining away, this liquid of inner death not made to see the light of day. Lucky day: the sprite picks a bouquet, held by the feet heads down, and a hare caught in her snares. She brings them to Gramma, who grumbles, groans and mutters filth, feathers, wood ticks, but carves faster than her shadow—the feathers for the pillows, the fur for the boots, nothing's wasted. The sprite has a noggin of rotten wheat, a head full of screwy straw of the old battle-axe; can't pray worth a damn; can't curtsy worth a damn; can't wash worth a damn. But as bold as a bitch, and the meat brightens up the monotony of the first snowfalls. Gramma plucks and slurps, slurps with pleasure when it's stew night of game birds killed in mid-flight.

There she goes, scooting off as soon as she's sated. Bowlegged little beast of the litter, but unkillable. Astride. The sprite burns the mongoloid by straddling him like a horse, though she's gone from light as a feather to a ton of bricks—he doesn't realize that she's grown like a heifer, fat in the hips and bee stings for breasts. The mongoloid blows steam, the redhead and Luke run in circles around them hooting and howling—and JJ must ride hard to chase the nor'easter and its little soft flakes—and it all ends ass over head in the field, in a heap of sweaty children. She, set up on three holes. Even in all the giant mess, the unforgettable three holes. Impossible to trample on her. You'd need to whip her with branches, train her in Petawawa. Not much more you can do now, it's a new century, Youth Protection, but it has to be said, Gramma thinks, those were the days.

The redhead is bedridden, ailing with consumption in the freezing cold at winter's end, and no one's slept for a fortnight, nightmared into his coughing spells. He lies in Gramma's room, looking sallow in the flame of the lantern burning day and night, in the stink of mustard poultices and urea, thyme tea and prayers, rubbing alcohol massaged on the soles of the feet to get the fever down. Usually, men die older in the country. This gives them hope.

The cough explodes like thunder imprisoned in the bed, amplified by the night and the four walls. The sprite tosses and turns in a nocturnal roll, sleeps one second at a time in the void between two thundering booms, roughs up her stinky doll, pillow and hooked rug to make a dam. How can you be alone in another's suffering? She goes down, just after three, to poke the logs, embers, pots and pans—a racket in the scullery—with the malicious wish to wake the male brood, those able to get some shut-eye in this shrine of spittle and mucus. The sprite eye-measures the gin toddy, the cobbler's recipe, with a generous spoonful of butter dropped in each of the three mugs. She grabs the handles. With each step she takes, the ceramic mugs clatter in her overfull hands, interrupting the prayers of Gramma, who raises an eyebrow. Three mugs? The sprite holds the redhead between two coughing fits, the grandmother pours the liquid, a descending slope into the ailing pharynx: one sip for Matthew, one sip for Gramma, one sip for Matthew, one sip for the sprite, one sip... The redhead zonks out at last, wheezing and hacking at the same time. A hoarse motor, a jammed starter, Gramma and the sprite burst out laughing. A rare laughter.

The sprite has a way of avoiding the chores and Gramma's spite: poaching. For the family, the urchins, for Gramma's gluttony, for the fun of it, the pleasure of sucking on bones. She sets off for the woods in the cool morning air, game bag swinging from her waist, disappears between the tree trunks and bony branches, scrawny like her. Whole days spent among the trees, Artemis with her slingshot, in a game of patience and discomfort. Waiting. Waiting until her spine moulds at last, liquid bones, to the knots, nests, bark and branchioles. She pisses standing up to see herself flow, yellow streams; her odour has changed, more like a hare than milk; and her hair grows like the spring moss in which she rolls until the dampness rises into her, unbearable, reaches her scalp, until it blisters holes in her skin, her cool willing flesh. She returns chilled to the bone at dusk with her bundle of dead animals and wood. She's learned how to pluck to avoid harsh complaints: she hasn't helped with the oats, the digging, the axing, the stitching, the soup, the chickens, the darning, the gardening, the sweeping, the kneading, the animals, the fire. The mongoloid hands her a few mouthfuls of stew with congealed fat on the sly, and an old carrot full of sprouts—it's springtime!—filched from the crate, and that's enough to hold her rumbling stomach through the night.

Straw hats, baseball caps, rubber boots. Tackle box: homemade flies of fallen bird feathers and two Joliette Hopper dry flies H12 bought in the village with JJ's pennies. Spoon baits, sinkers, penknives passed down from fathers. The mongoloid doesn't fly-fish but digs around for worms, anyways, sun's coming out, gonna be too hot soon. You can find the fishing basket by the scent; and the one with cucumbers, apples and coarse salt. They divvy up the gear by size, the older ones drag the heavy stuff, the brat gropes the rods, and the brood John-Jude Luke James Matthew Peter-Joseph the sprite gets cracking, hobbling along, the toes of some stepping on the heels of others. A steam train trying to get momentum, hoarsely chug-chugging along.

Past the road, the barn. Past the barn, the vegetable garden. Gramma is weeding, knees in the soil. Straw hat, gum boots, gloves, flesh of the son, and the brood brushes past her, forcing the undeniable family portrait. Nothing to be done but merge into it, anyways. Gramma drives the spade into the soil, loosens the joints and brings up the rear. Make haste, the fish won't wait past noon. The mongoloid screams with joy. You could call it a family. Or a seven-headed monster.

The best fly-fishing is at Ass Lake—Lord knows. Village talk claims that a toothless old-timer lost its *b* and the name got passed down ever since. After the Little Chinese Girls River, take a left. There you have to step over rocks, the water high with rain from the night before, you'll get wet for sure. Like happy pigs in the jam, the brood charges in. The brat goes flying in the water, pushed in, goodbye cucumbers apples and cap. The siblings dislocate their jaws, but Gramma lags behind on the shore, stalled. They carry on, without a word. They carry on and each has time to imagine a return to normal: the children on one bank, the grandmother on the other. Young. Old. To each their shore. JJ takes action. He drops his load—tackle box and stinky basket—recrosses the current, jumping from stone to stone with the same light bounce as a startled deer in the forest. Wasting no time, he bends over, puts his beefy face through Gramma's skirts, stands up slowly with all the strength of his man's body not yet dead and carries her across the river, the grandmother perched on his shoulders.

Perched on the shoulders of the dead sister's son, on a Sunday under a cloudy sky pierced by more and more rays of light, tall like an allegorical doll, long like a St. Jean puppet, Gramma bursts out laughing. Thunderous joy, quickly filed away in the heads of the cerberus brood. JJ completes his portage, one careful step at a time, walking directly in the water so as to not lose his footing, pants soaked to the thigh. Gurgles of air escape from his rubber boots, adding an aqueous touch to the birdsong and the children's amazement. Gramma gently gets down from JJ's shoulders. The siblings remain with their mouths wide open, now they're the ones stalled, while Gramma chomps at the bit. A pretty picture, something to make you smile. Anyways, Gramma says, we're not here to dry out. Let's go.

In the shade of the willow by Ass Lake, the mongoloid plays the kazoo with a blade of grass held between his thumbs. He learned from Gramma, who used to play duets with Violet, Violet of before, when Gramma used to smile. The whole brood knows how to whistle like woodchucks. JJ fingers in his yap. The redhead in trills, Mozart tunes caught on the radio. The mongoloid, his symphony no. 3 for the flies and sunrise. The sprite and the brat playing his students, glued to him like choirboys. It drags on, disharmony for a quackgrass orchestra, while the rest work on napping or rock skipping. The sprite loses interest, fidgets, knots, braids, plaits fragile grass effigies, amulets with dandelion faces and green-wheat arms. The redhead catches ladybugs for her, squishing them to make eyes. Good-luck charms. Fresh dolls that don't stink, still supple, not starched by two generations of dried damp kisses.

Gramma slurps with pleasure when it's Ass Lake chowder night, and in her devouring, her lips soften, her face loses its ravenous wicked faerie godmother look.

The sprite is more than ten fingers old. No head, Gramma says, but the devil on two feet and monsters with tails hot on her heels. Forced to lose herself between the moon and her trees—we're not in the city, no whining that there's nothing to do in St. Mother of Vinegar—the sprite sparkles and grows, quicksilver, slipping like water between your fingers, all legs and long limbs, made of just a few—five or six—drops good enough to slurp. Gangly, sprouted like a whip: a batrachian thinness, ephemeral arms and legs. Forced to sway her hips, kneecaps and elbows protruding, she's constantly clumsy and prone to labyrinthitis. All kneecaps and elbows. And yet even if bony, she's starting to grow into a woman, by what magic, what sorcery?

From wild child with short sweet clover braids to huntress with a gold sling is just one step. One, two, three! Red Light! Green Light! Chores turn into games. Where is the fissure that makes adulthood put an end to fun? Not here.

Let's not make a scene about the first monthlies: one day, it leaks, it's red, and your stomach deflates into your crotch. One day, you start scrubbing your skivvies with homemade soap, hands chilled to the bone, coz hot water sets the stain. Gramma's napkins and the sprite's dry out on the line, and watching them wrestle in the wind, the grandmother thinks that it's been a long time, a really long time, since someone's come to fetch her to help out with a birthing. A sign of the times? Of old age?

Half-chick, half-grasshopper, dumb girl, the sprite continues to run after the seven rains, trouble and storms. In her own bedroom—the boys sleep together in the big room—her desire grows, a primordial joy, this other kind of child hunger, immense, that brews under the new hair and flesh. She dreams of eating boys eating snuggles, eating everything, everyone, Joe, Jacob, Jerome—creating others, getting out of the family—a tartare with rosemary and chervil, yum. She stuffs her pillow between her legs, and the rough pleasure turns gentle. She laughs, quietly.

She swings by the village mid-hunt, slingshot at her belt, hangs around the church steps. She attracts children like flies. They come in droves for their shooting lesson, pockets stuffed with stones. They follow her to the cemetery, where they line up bottles and cans on the gravestones. The racket and shattering glass rouse the older ones. They sniff her out from a distance, the Jeromes, Jacobs, Joes. She does the same, checks them out from a distance. Then she gets going, returns to the forest—and the others in tow, and those of tomorrow, and she as well. From afar, they're carried along, borne by the nor'easter, floating almost all the way to the house, joined by their desire. And she discovers the joy, the heat, of losing oneself in the eyes of another. A good girl? Wise? No. Wild, a whirlwind, dissolute to the max.

It's gonna get worse, the more she skips church, Gramma thinks, slurping with pleasure familyless in her pew, next to the Thomassins mother and daughter, thinking of the stew awaiting her after mass.

The sprite's fingers seek other gestures besides getting chapped in the dishwater, the Hail-Marys-full-of-grace, the silent piano or the bleaching. She dreams of fleeing to the lilacs, the boys, the raspberries. Plays the scatterbrain, learned it all from the mongoloid, knows how to avoid getting into a jam for exuberant Sundays alone.

Gramma bites her lips, watching the sprite throwing herself at men. The sprite who's looking for Eden limbo fire love the foreseen thing. Gramma waits for her, and for misfortune too. It's her mouth that she sees first on the sprite's face, unbearable, her reneged mouth, the one stolen from God and more than foretold. Her mouth of memories, when she used to laugh.

The sprite is thirteen. She sees clearly. What she feels, she knows. She sees the guilt-ridden ones with their post-sex tristesse, all those against the body, against nature, she sees it in everyone, the chains and tethers. It burns her. And she sees Gramma too, lashing out, in her mind. Gramma's waiting for the prophesy, waiting to see the sprite join the military ranks of flesh and fresh fillies: waiting for her to return dried out, old; for her to return erased if not dead, like all women: of shame, rape, anemia, famine, TB, Pythia, family, restraint, embarrassment, hate, silence, dead from stitching, breastfeeding, ass-wiping, dead at the bottom of the lake, foot caught in the trap, ring on the finger—living dead like all the others all the same. Dead from living. Like all women.

You'll see, Gramma says between tight lips. Time will put her in the ranks. She'll grow old, the arrogant one. She'll dry up, like we've all done from grandmother to daughter from caveman times. She'll see, live, shut up, die. Killed. Like me, fuck, like all women.

She's thirteen, the sprite, and her first rootword rings clear, her first word, her true love. No. No. Who will be will know, who will know will see and what I'll be will wart.

She cuts a large square out of the moth-eaten and piss-stained hooked rug to make a bundle. Throws in a lock of the mongoloid's hair, a squint, some tarragon, a handful of ashes and echoes, the stinky doll: her escape journal. She doesn't say goodbye, slips out through the window and leaves for the city, the city of adults. Escaping with her life, in an instant, an instant and

absence.

IV

"she had told the sprite to be prepared"

My God, it's full of stars! the sprite whispers, dazzled, stepping on the sidewalk, strolling in the city dumbfounded. The city: flaxen conglomeration of lights, and sequins floating in the haze—so then the city, such magic!, can fly?—sequins connected by electrical streaks, pulsating in a vast red, purple, blue grid… The sprite absorbs thirty billion watts. The halo radiating from the centre, the centre emitting an aureole, warms her all the way here—such heat! such magic!—and like a will-o'-the-wisp entices and inhales her. Her brow, her cheek, her dishevelled mane are sucked in by this aerial milk. And her face turns inside out like a glove until only the lips remain; lips and kisses; aspiration; and she wets her howling flesh. The sprite hoots with joy under the flashing sparks, in a sublime dissolving. Welcome to the city.

The noises here are so different from the octaves of the cardinals and trills of the chickadees. And yet so familiar: church bells, car horns, voices automated in her blockskull, similar to the turbulent white noise she heard as a fetus, the strong sleet of her mother's blood, the echoing and syncopated clamour that followed her in her closed cast-iron chamber. Muffled sonar, pulsar of limbs to the limbic system—so far so close so strong. And now in the city, the feedback, response and resonance, sonorous, amplified, amalgamated. The sounds crash and stick like liquid clay against her skull and neck, in front of her face: they forge a disguise, and she cries tears of joy beneath this mask. At last! The source of sensations is at once herself, so far so close so strong, and outside herself. At last! She is a huntress in an intimate hideout, her face and features camouflaged. The city's noises—like embers!—become those of her thoughts, their branches and bronchioles crackle and burn like her skull of burnt birch. The city's noises are great lullabies, chants of courage saying my love, my sweet sweet girl, go, live.

Flying streetcars everywhere, open-top busses, ten-storey double-deckers, shimmering drones, hot-air balloons; and people, people, people. She's in the nosebleed seats, spends nights, the first, the following ones, on one bus ticket getting the princess tour of Surreality, a merry-go-round, legs stretched on the seat, a dazzled riding somnambulist, nose in the sky. Her eyes like saucers from fatigue blend her dreams with the city, constellations with pointillist serpentine conurbations. She goes cross-eyed. The hum of industrial oxygen lulls her to sleep. The sprite rests from levitation, a mechanical buoyancy she can't get used to. It'll come with time. But for the moment her distaff body wants to move: walk, jump, run, fall over in suspension. She's constantly shocked. The impassive crowd smirks seeing her—aaaahhh! these people from the north-south-west, country folk, unable to forget their legs, limbs, unable to simply let themselves move in absence.

She feeds on neon, water from the fountain and the green sun rolls from King o' the Main, adding bitter leaves—dandelion, scraggly sprigs and plantains, barely sprouted yet there, you just have to know how to look—which she also uses to make dolls. Small grass effigies with faces full of sun, two soot stains for eyes. She sells them like snake oil liniment for three pennies, in parks where kids come to romp around, do pirouettes and cartwheels, straddle and play war. Thanks to her silver tongue, the sprite gets set up with two families, playing clown for the kids off and on while the parents go dancing. Nannies are for the rich. The sprite has ten leather fingers to suckle, she inspires a countryside confidence. And scraping by amuses her, as long as it's free, and full of holes.

Life is a spectacle. Astride on the roof of the skyscraper church—she climbs up what's a fire escape or maintenance stairs for the tiles and bells, who knows—feet dangling in the void, next to the glimmering purple cross, she remains fascinated by others, all the others who effortlessly stream past, ten metres above the ground, on inflatable sidewalks, fascinated by their colourful masks sounds lights. Glorious fauna of barn owls, a Sunday fauna: buskins, scyllas and sombreros; the nowhere women of Christmas in sequins, spangles, triple false eyelashes, curlers and spacesuits; the skinheads on stilettos, bearded kids, bleached-hair albinos, the muzhiks in crinolines, the topless with faux leather implants, virtual flying bears, hygienic sebum, ermines pumped with B Negative, the pompadours and mohawks, the car salesmen, the strippers, the tattooed at sun-up, all before this young oh so young hungry careless loose tigress who bursts out laughing My God, it's full of stars!

A lullaby rises to her lips, come from who knows where? An intimate throat song singing of six stillborn males, two late-born daughters, one dead Snow, men gone like flies, and wise midwives from mother to daughter. The sprite rips an arm off the effigy, holds the blade of grass between her thumbs and replays the melody on the urban kazoo. She strings her notes for the storeys and stars, wondering whether JJ and the mongoloid are already dead—they're the right age for it—whether that would explain the interstellar silence, the absent responses to her postcards, the house's silence.

The house. She hears herself think. And it doesn't fall on deaf ears.

A provincial symphony no. 3 for the sun and flies, genealogical blares magically infused by faerie fingers city fingers: five notes, five, like the scent of soil, like the chirping of fledglings, ponderous, prophetic, five notes laughed and cried all at once that shake in echoes of luminous streaks, that pulsate amplified by the feedback pump. She starts again, with gusto. Someone stops and turns his mask toward her, toward this well of false notes and music. One second, a single one, quickly gone, and him gone back, snatched by his daily meander like a branch fallen in the river. But the sprite saw it. She saw the redirecting of the eyes, the moment of attention, the listening. One second, a single one. And a minuscule fracture fissured, oh so finely, on the last note, her city wolf.

She returns to the square every evening to put on a show, sitting on the church steps. The guys circle around her. She follows those who follow her, a carousel, practises kissing, barbaric kisses, the kind that remain and resonate *in front*, always *in front* of the face, in this clamorous mask imposed by the city, where lips collide and tongues resonate in stereo, and the eardrums painfully vibrate. Mouth noises. You'd think you were in an aquarium. It annoys her to be caught in her facial mask, irritated by the interstices impossible, always impossible to fully fill, by the wind blowing between her and the other, the sou'wester face that stops her from reading the pores. And fucking? Another story. A story of no more rump or gristle, only shitting or finding something to feed the mouth and the belly. The sprite comes, makes them come and returns to the chaos, like backwash.

She unconsciously hums the stillborns and her mother

the absent one, breathes them, drop by drop of awkward memories, on her stem of grass. A lullaby she repeats like a tic on and on in a strange land. She crosses the park and, drawn by the emptiness, plays the notes even louder. Curious looks. The sprite sings, why not? She blares out the mongoloid, the fifth one who only half counts, and the brat in the grimy water. A kid in a halogen mask, smiling ear to ear, gets down from the floating sidewalk and follows in her footsteps, like a brother, a city rat. He shadows her, unsteady on his feet but not losing the rhythm. She laughs and relaunches the refrain. Twins join in to extend the train, hand in hand. The sprite sings the doll with the iron eyes and a mane of horsehair, Ass Lake, Deadman River. The feedback harmonizes, calling children to join the line. Awkward steps become drumbeats. A stunningly shoddy troupe. Merry parents start following at a distance, faltering. The sprite has fun, first and last, cradle and all, sings her blasted motet and all the serialism of boys turned dead. Kids line up behind her, centipede-like. The concrete resonates in the echoing bunker like a glass drum in a cast-iron chamber. It vibrates until the material responds, and cracks, a mask splits here, there, the marble walls of a skyscraper. The joy of collapsing, of being strangers together.

When out of breath she closes her lips at last, a legion lags behind her, a joyful thousand-headed monster. A staggering battalion of kids' noggins and chaos. And the adults, how beautiful when they smile!—the masks vibrate—the pierced Blacks in full colour, the Debbys in heat, griffins in the flesh, piratesses in bonnets, crackheads, metal princesses, Nunavut futurists, beautiful, beautiful to connect since we're all splendours in the sudden silence, splendours in the hushing of the thousand-mouth chorus, in the all-engulfing silence, the constant sonorous sludge, motors and motets, timbres, chimes, pulsars, in the engulfing silence we are a rare asonia. And the masks crack like the concrete all around, revealing thin lines of white flesh, so snowy white beneath, hidden for such a long time—for such a long time absent, covered under a shell.

That was the first day. Three thousand six hundred others will follow. They will make the sprite into a queen. A Mameluke dancer with a grass kazoo, a revolutionary.

"I jump into the ring
my love I'll never heal
if you screw me in my wound"

You can already feel that noon'll be a scorcher, you can feel it and know it. The sprite, hands on the steering wheel, receives dull blows, shaken by the jolts of the potholes on the big hill. The landscape inundates her—tarragon of haystacks, drought, dung, the odours infuse her, invade the car in tangible lurches. The childhood spent in St. Mother of Vinegar of Laurentia comes back to her in fits and starts, great armfuls of aromas: pine, musk, manure and wheat. Travel bag on the passenger's seat, a strip of the hooked rug—all that remains, so threadbare—tied to the handle, a colourful signal on the baggage carousel, the bag seems like an ogre when she remembers leaving in the opposite direction, little plush bear with a child's modest bundle. The bundle, so small. And she also. A sudden violent lurch and she smacks her elbow in the door right on the funny bone. She curses, goddammit, no washing the mouth out with soap, no one to hold back the outbursts, the excesses. Showing up unexpectedly in the light of day. She hasn't told them.

The sprite. How ironic now, this name that endures despite her slender limbs, the unframable lengths, her figure of sharp angles reminiscent of a calm grasshopper, or a praying mantis. The names come back to her as the places roll past the window. The forest of the Hangwoman Tree, where the river and its swimmable soup flow—the water hole called Jezebel. After the cow fields, the parcel of land named Belle de Jour, inexplicably situated between the fifth and sixth parcels. And after turning left, there, at the end of the gravel road that you need to know where to look to see, that you need to feel in the dark to find, there, greyer and smaller than the one sketched in memory, the house. The house where she was born, where the sprite comes from. The nest, known since forever, the arena of love.

She stops, kills the engine. She knows that machine noises are rare enough around here that she doesn't need to honk. Sweat pours down her spine, what heat. The door opens onto a black hole. Exactly just before noon, and her dark flashes of recollection.

The grandmother appears. Still svelte from sadness, muscular from working to feed herself, white hair, strong legs. Strong from having become a grandmother, a grandmother at thirty-seven, a short time ago once upon a time not so long ago, when in the beginning was the word, and from not having, once the boys became men ready for dying, more mouths to feed, more knuckles to slap with her tough hand, more litanies, more broods to round up before the stew got cold. She looks, and against the bright sunlight, recognizes. It is said, written, gospel word: first and last, cradle and all. The only one to return because the only one returnable, unkillable. Gramma unclenches her lips, a breath escapes, almost nothing, a miasma, tension letting go. She turns and goes back into the house, leaves the door wide open to the flies the chirping crickets. It's an invitation, the only welcome possible here. Shouldn't ask for more. The sprite enters the black hole, the square eye of the needle: a return to the shadows—the birth of it all—and to all the rest.

Which one came back unexpectedly? The one who rediscovers the foundations of childhood—structures of love happiness hardship thoughts laughter tears—or the one who is supposed to be tough, a wretch, the worst, wasting the perfect lineage of dying upright, wasting the hard-won solitude. Which one?

The sprite rediscovers the walls of her childhood, and it all slaps her in the face. The hints of cedar, the cinders, the dust piled up between the floorboards. She falls back into a state in which the air and tissues were caressing hands and all surroundings were loved; the silky surroundings of the self, of simply being, being alive. She feels her body melt into the panelling, the horse, the wood stove, the mongoloid,

the absence, oceanic orgasm, without however ceding the boundaries of her body to this devouring.

Gramma is there, leaning against the table, arms crossed. Huge and primordial, heavy with her dead her men her flies her rosary her ladybugs for Christ's sake her fuck her wrinkles around the mouth. A witch, the sprite wonders. Glaring gorgons from mother to daughter, first and last? Fuck, the sprite answers. Home sweet home. It's hotter than hell's kitchen, chervil and rosemary, spirals practically emanate from her sweating skin. The sprite strips, from head to foot, voila, stark naked, right back where she started in grandmother's eyes, with pubic hair. From now on, woman to woman, from now on, we, mismatched and the same. Equal.

This return, this exhibition, this branding with the red-hot iron of the first day is what the sprite feels, she knows the power of history in the bones. She returns to the source, the pulsating house, movement. She comes back to find her ground. A salmon leaping upstream. She knows, though young she already knows, that she'll turn into a witch, no other fate told by the spite or time past than that of worm-eaten raspberries and who will be will wart. No, no, no. Returning to the ailinghouse of ailinglove, returning to her, to Gramma the devouress: this is the only way to turn the tide in advance.

The first days pass and stack up easily, like firewood under the stairs. It's a geometric dance, a moving architecture of pure bodies sharing space, the grown-up sprite and Gramma in their female house. Matters of the body, in the daily accumulation of animated insignificant gestures, each for herself—coffee dishes meals navigational movements reading napping washing, and for the grandmother praying rosary in hand—without brushing against each other, without agreeing to the other's presence, so far so close so strong that it's already a sign of recognizing, sharing smells and animal routes.

The childhood house is remade in the present moment: no more tornadoes or cacophony of objects, no more calling out to feed, no John-Jude Luke James Matthew Peter-Joseph the sprite waltzing in three times a day. Now, it would be calling on the dead.

The sprite feels, she knows that she can't, has never been able to touch Gramma. There's a risk that she who's held herself up for so long with tough talk, tense body and no gentleness might crack. The sprite doesn't go near her, makes a decoction of cherry stems, pours it as an offering and leaves it within reach, picks up the empty cup later. The gesture ends there. Everything in St. Mother of Vinegar has the luxury of stopping. Through the window, the sprite watches time passing— the animals grazing, Gramma, out of the frame, tilling—the tic-tac of chanting crickets that turn, at owl's light, into croaking bullfrogs. Infancy and idleness dissolve into each other, penetrate the sprite's pores. She goes up to the second floor, for the umpteenth nap, full of languor for the umpteenth time. Her bedroom, now so small, the walls so closed in, like a comfortable coffin. She turns around, takes three steps: in the boys' dormitory, the stink of scalps, fisticuffs and brute sleep lingers. The tiny window radiates—a sun hole of memories. The house breathes; its creaks crack the restraint, and the sprite, force-fed with memories, the return of sensations, masturbates frantically all at once, as quietly as possible, standing up against the closed door of the boys' room, comes immediately, comes with the solar speed of the solitary orgasm that remains one of her great, great secrets.

The sprite roams the fields, marks her territory once more, walks barefoot in the quackgrass clover thistles plantains dandelions, joyously scrapes her ankles and the soles of her feet, runs on gravel to toughen her calluses. Days pass and she gets lighter and faster. Days pass by the dozen and the sprite becomes tree, field, cow once more, polymorphic in the landscape. She slips naked in the frog pond, swims lazily. Awash on the surface, water spiders and white larvae form a restless constellation, a phosphorescent nuclear dance that reminds her of liver spots, the motionless and magnificent moles on the back of Gramma's hands.

She's happier here, in St. Mother of Vinegar of Laurentia, even in the midst of family spite and of what made her, in the midst of her people, they are mine as I am theirs, even though many have become memories. The fruit, the apple, the tree. Anywhere else—my limbs, my limbo, my plague—the sprite would've been, she feels it and knows it, just another pocket effigy, a frayed faerie, perhaps a queen, the first and last, half nothing.

Dried by sun and wind, the sprite can't help but remember remember to slam the door. The missing names of the brood resonate in the hole left by the silence. The semi-darkness is refreshing, a balm, and the play of shadows draws Gramma's silhouette in the rocking chair to the right of the wood stove: neck broken at a sharp angle, a black heron. Collapsed, head in her hands, her shoulder blades shaken by quick breaths—sobs? Yes. The old woman's crying. Her wrinkles fade in her hands, she cries stale bread, grimy crusts, she cries her ossuary face turned mask from solitude, and when she—oh, barely!—raises her face from her palms, she sees her features there, dissolved, fine gloves of sheer silk covering fingers and lifelines, her face melted in her hands, her face fleeing in morphological coulees to the floor: lava of sad, heavy drops of her. She cries, decomposing tear by tear, her face flowing between the floorboards, slipping between the soot and frass, the rosary beads, wonders, dust mites, nothing.

The sprite sits down at the grandmother's feet, places a hand on her knee. The sprite touches Gramma. She leaves her hand on the knee. Gramma doesn't raise her eyes. She'll never hit again, never again. The sprite places her head on this hand. An angel passes, a fly buzzes. Gramma cries, inconsolable. From the old woman, sadness rains, rancid, the old woman's slough, the ice of long-time spite. The sprite places a kiss, almost nothing, a breath on the knee. Yes. The skin is soft, the sobs long. Yes. Her head finds the kneecap, leans on it. Another eternity, an icon, all sadness. Witches, witches, they'll call them, but love and nest for her. For the women, spite reversed, negative life, chosen life. Chosen. The sprite kisses the knee again. And again. Point-blank. In a slowness untouched by time. She runs kisses halfway up the thigh. Her closed fists knead, wanting to soften and split, massaging the muscle fibres, untangling the darkness, pulling with great finger bites, taking large gulps of the white inner thighs. The breaths increase; the sobs diminish. The sprite returns to her source, no cotton, no dam to stop her; and the old ogress of pumice stone, lava and brambles sheds with the force of being licked there, she contracts. The grandmother falls in water, abandons her life of failure and faith. The sprite eats mother and absence, eats mother of mother. She licks, overflowing with mouth and saliva, labial vocalizations similar to those when learning to speak, forging with lips with tongues the perimeter of the pit, sculpting the silence in another, in another way. Now Gramma flows from below, unravels in quivering sighs, bestial syllables, exhalations and monumental moans. All restraint gone to the dogs; joyous moaning; wordless wallowing; hands wet with secretions: cannibal devouring and chameleon before nightfall—she and she—a purification to pleasure in the abrasion of the ligneous body, a glorious fountain lapped up by a medusa offshoot, shatter-masks and a thousand words. A fountain of ravishment. Equal, babbling in babble, in the primal time of love, they are raptured from consolation to daring to terror, to the original mystery: when Gramma climaxes.

No more talk, nothing tough, nothing. No more origin or beginning or end. Not even the word. Because from language prophecies come, yes, and interdictions; the vast before-us. So they remain beyond words, yes, on the floor, two women entwined together, willingly mute, their ravished faces, pure, reduced to living tissues; and pulsing, pumped up from below to the fixed fontanelle, a sublime joy—music slow splendours of milk and the dead—eroding their faces and making them new. Witches witches. Devoured raw, escaped alive, goddesses wonders harpies, collapsed in the dust, remade and spent, at the original birth, the first time of love ailinglove, and of its hatred, reversed.

The great, unexpected hunger of a world's beginning, the same found in embracing infants: the hunger of baby teeth for the elastic flesh, so supple, offering no resistance to the mouth (lips teeth tongue stomach throat). Supreme softness, a feeding call, flesh of progeny. The orgy of devouring granted, blood, viscera and honey, increasing the milk the butter, infinitely. Each other's fangs, lips and tongues on the other's flesh, the sprite and the old woman.

I had become a statue, Gramma says, a skeleton. A long time passed, a long time in terms of milk, in terms of ass, in terms of hunger.

Now days are vertical, spent doing small chores, kneading and making bread, trimming basil and mint, sipping herbal teas; spent scampering in the woods, slingshot at the belt, walking under a sky eviscerated by the sun or under warm showers; soil-blacked feet, filthy nails, Sunday game birds, the days pass. The sprite and the old woman, like needles of the compass, keep a respectable distance between their bodies in the house. But nights bring them together, and the devouring begins again, this great, great secret: tongues, voraciousness, sticky wet fingers, magnificent raptures, dissolution, sharing fed by strength, pure joy, pure power, orgasms.

That was the first year. Three thousand six hundred others will follow. They will make the sprite into woman, tempest, forest, faerie; and Gramma into sky, and breath, and faerie. First and first.

Spooning on the bed, the sprite a head taller, nestled against the mother backbone until she turns into a bird of hope: returning to her eggs, to the ivory of the sacred spine, turning into a fetus in her own lumbar vertebrae.

The little fuck of a sprite has become queen; a great dirty queen, like the river, mountain, rocks. She is a rebellious frond. From hunting, she's learned how to change her sweat, a chameleon, into the scent of nettles and peat of St. Mother of Vinegar. It's magic: the electric-blue petals of chicory flit up to her skull, crown of flowers, thorns or Medusa's mane. The sprite is haloed. Wicked faerie godmother ripped out at the roots, she drew on the power, without blasphemous curses. The first. The air, grass, foliage, bark, the ghosts of the men dead like flies— everything around her, animal vegetal horizon, is like an enveloping fabric, like loving hands; all the inseparable landscape is like silk to her. Everything, and the other as well: her grandmother, her source.

Candle in hand, flame flickering, the sprite advances carefully, one step at a time, to enter the black hole of the socket. She lifts the fragile flame and sees: the milky white zenith of bone is magnificent! She is inside Gramma's cranium: left eye the threshold of migraines, dead sea in ripples of bone. She presses on, goes deeper. She feels the deep rolling breaths. The eye-nose-mouth crucifix reveals itself in the glow of what she's seen will see: children, infants, men gone and dead, the great woman of unrigidified love, metamorphosed rosary love, she sees, she feels and knows. Gramma is at death's door.

Already. There's no small pleasure that doesn't end all too soon.

The sprite kneels on the wood floorboards of the kitchen, while Gramma lies, livid and weakened, on a moth-eaten mite-bitten hooked rug handed down from mother to daughter. Water boils on the back burner of the wood stove, for herbal tea and for sponging the ailing body, once so strong. Not much life is left, it smells more like a corpse than like love. The wood stove door is open, the fire crackles, the cinders pop, warming up the old bones. Gramma is dying, such sadness. She murmurs something very slowly and the sprite listens to the ponderous, prophetic, oracular words, listens to the last telling, the last telling of her life. Gramma says:

was
born older than
my mother was born
in the time before and I've
grown simpler from death to death
until I became mother of my mother
and the vertiginous hidden side of music

and
I hope
through you love
centuries strength a meteor shower

I opened
my entrails
three times a miracle!
and bore the emptiness that followed spite
there you will read the future and its ravishing devourings
there read the matryoshka mothers and queens since we have
I tell you we have the art of sleeping
in upheaval

am
we
all women
great faerie beasts
snuffed out reborn returned
rebreathed and swallowed by staggered centuries
the first mouth will be the last
kissing you

if
milk
leaves me
my femurs
become liquid
catch me liquid I flow
faerie siren in milky streams, Cleopatra—queen at last!
gone with the calves cows
and the bathwater

spread
the wings
first and first
I become glacial
and know how to
conquer gods and
harpies, and eagles
iron letters, be the last
foundational daughter, let's be arms
together and slingshot mouths and pearlhearts
let's disgorge be pure distress, witches, tongues and
fangs of empresses together, together in the pleasure of collapses

rejoin
Snow sparks Bengali
embers I burn at the Perseids
meteor shower summer shower lightning
the energy contained in not having disappeared
before, not having—what joy!—disappeared before
disappearing

Adele
my love
go howl God
go and become cyclone
clamour singular music flour
and milk before making us dead go
give an eye for an eye from our heads to the skies
go and become scream before sigh before muffled before flesh

go
my love
piercing horse
for pleasure and orchestra
be golden blasphemies thunder
echo chamber go be avalanche and—have mercy!—
swallow me with the calves cows Snow butter ogresses
riding hoods and throw up the bones, the others

we
will have
survived God
all the things they said about us
our tongue is memory and what our heart used to be
when it was crown

and
the hand
of words
pierced our hearts
to caress you queen and
who loves me follows me beyond this motherdeath hole
the hand
of words
caressed our heart
and who loves me follows me
speaks me beyond this motherdeath hole

love
go

"I dreamt of being a girl"

— Josée Yvon (1950–1994)

Salutations to all from whom I borrowed,
D. Kimm, Geneviève Desrosiers, Hélène Monette, Josée Yvon.

Translator's Coda

The Faerie Devouring is written in a genre that purposely escapes definition. Is it a timeless fairy tale or harsh realism, you may wonder. A coming-of-age story vaguely set in the rural Quebec of the 1950s or a futuristic incantation? A feminist howling or a fearless telling of an era's prejudices? And the beautiful fact is that it is all of these and more.

So, the great challenge (and joy) of writing this translation was finding (and inventing) in English the various linguistic registers and music through which Lalonde's book sings: the language of fables, sorcery, science, Catholicism, the sensory language of environments, bodies, and sexual desire, the rhythms of nursery rhymes, lullabies, and spells, the colour and specificity of regional expressions, the parlance of the mid-twentieth century, and the imagined vernacular of the future. The book is also suffused with phrases and echoes from other Quebec writers—weaving yet another layer into the fabric of its linguistic registers—as well as neologisms, word play, and double entendres. The language is fierce, raw, even crude at times, and exuberant, imaginative, and limitless at other times.

The lacunae in the narrative or lack of fussy explanations are counterbalanced by the book's echoing structure and its carefully considered, sensory, phonic language. Seeking to reveal and challenge, but also possibly to disturb and cast a spell, the book bends the rules and demands that I—as its reader, translator, writer—bend them too, exposing the sometimes-life-or-death necessity of stretching the limits of the possible.

The Faerie Devouring is a bold book and this is partly what compelled me to translate it, right from when I first opened Lalonde's *La dévoration des fées*, for we urgently need bold and risk-taking books, now more than ever.

ABOUT THE AUTHOR

Catherine Lalonde is a poet, spoken word artist, and journalist. Among her four published books, *Corps Étranger* won the Émile Nelligan Award in 2009 and *La dévoration des fées* (*The Faerie Devouring*) was awarded le prix Alain-Grandbois de l'Académie des lettres du Québec and was a finalist for a 2018 Governor General's Literary Award. Having trained at the Ateliers de Danse Moderne de Montréal, she has danced with Fondation Jean-Pierre Perreault, Michèle Rioux, Karina Iraola, and Jean-Sébastien Lourdais. She choreographed *Musica Nocturna*, a dance, theatre, and poetry piece, for Danse-Cité and the Festival International de la Littérature in 2009. Lalonde also works as a journalist and art critic for the Montreal daily *Le Devoir*.

ABOUT THE TRANSLATOR

Montreal-based poet, translator, and artist **Oana Avasilichioaei** has published five poetry collections, including *Expeditions of a Chimaera* (with Erín Moure; 2009), *We, Beasts* (2012; winner of the A.M. Klein Prize for Poetry) and *Limbinal* (2015). Previous translations include Bertrand Laverdure's *Universal Bureau of Copyrights* (2014; shortlisted for the 2015 ReLit Awards), Suzanne Leblanc's *The Thought House of Philippa* (co-translated with Ingrid Pam Dick; 2015), and Daniel Canty's *Wigrum* (2013). Her translation of Bertrand Laverdure's *Readopolis* won the 2017 Governor General's Literary Award for Translation.

COLOPHON

Manufactured as the first English edition of *The Faerie Devouring*
in the fall of 2018 by Book*hug.

Distributed in Canada by the Literary Press Group: lpg.ca

Distributed in the US by Small Press Distribution: spdbooks.org

Shop online at bookthug.ca

BOOK
PRODUCTION
WAR ECONOMY
STANDARD

Copy-edited by Stuart Ross
Type + design by Tree Abraham